Little Princesses

Princess Sucha's Cat

Aleix Cabrera

Illustration: Rocio Bonilla

WINDMILL BOOKS

"Do I have to be a real princess?" little Sucha asks herself. People from the court always tell her that princesses don't run, shout, wear clothes they like, or behave like she does.

3

Hmmm . . .

4

"If you carry on like that, you'll never become a queen," they scold her. Then Sucha looks at herself in the mirror doubtfully and glances at the garden. She asks herself why princesses can't climb trees or build tree houses in them like the **other children do.**

She wants to play too.

One day, Sucha receives

a mysterious present. It is well wrapped and there is a note hanging from it that says: "We hope that this new friend will show you the path you must follow. Do the same as him and there will be no princess better than you."

When she opens the box, the girl finds a Siamese cat. Before she has time to pick it up, the animal jumps out, lets out a musical meow, and runs off with such elegance that **Sucha is left very surprised.**

meow . . .

9

The cat walks, stops, and licks its coat. It is proud and clean by nature. Sucha realizes that these are two characteristics that a princess should have.

slurp . . .

slurp . . .

slurp . . .

The future queen decides to take a royal bath,
surrounded with toys and soap bubbles.
Then she tries to brush her hair as her mother
would do, but only manages to tangle her hair

even more **terribly.**

Giving up on her hairdo,

Sucha observes that her new friend has gray fur,
as smooth and soft as silk.
"I need an appropriate dress," she exclaims,
proud of her discovery.

pfffffff...

Sucha begins rummaging through all the wardrobes in the palace, but she can't find a dress she likes. Before giving up, she finds what she is looking for in the library.

"That red velvet curtain **would make the perfect dress for a princess.**"

Now the cat is tiptoeing

between Sucha's legs. It does so respectfully and with movements that appear to be almost a dance.

"If only I hadn't given up dance classes. Would I be able to move like that?" she asks herself.

To walk on tiptoes like the little cat, Sucha decides to put on her mother's high-heeled shoes. They go *clack-clack* as she walks. **"I seem more like a hen than a cat," she sighs sadly.**

"Maybe if I put socks

over the shoes, the heels won't tap with every step," she murmurs. And Sucha, who wants to be a refined princess, does so.

clack-clack!

Finally, with the socks pulled over the high-heeled shoes, the long curtain converted into a dress, her hair completely tangled, and a little soap behind her ears, Sucha decides to surprise the king and queen. She walks through the garden, **skipping and bowing.**

But Sucha does not manage it.

Unable to walk slowly, she stumbles and falls into the bushes. Boom! From the shock, the king and the queen almost end up with their tea and cakes on their hats. The court painter gets distracted and paints a large moustache on his assistant.

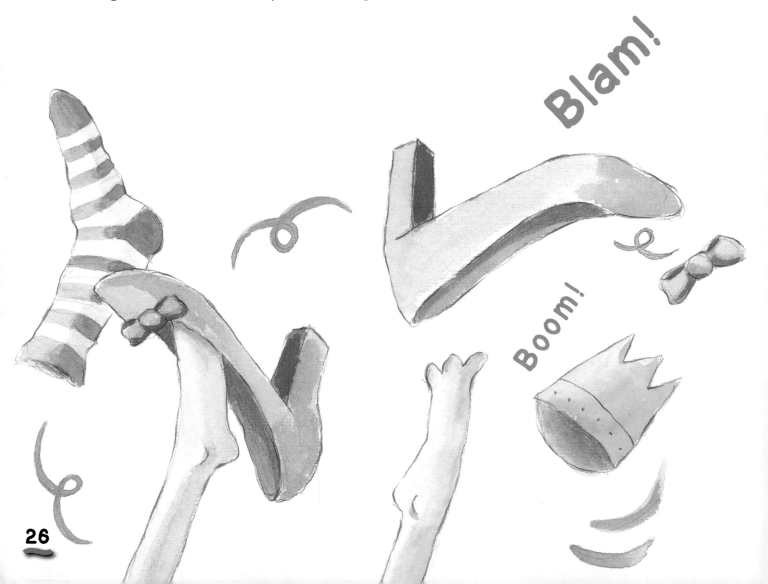

Blam!

Boom!

The cat, also surprised, runs rapidly, jumps over the railings of the veranda, and climbs up the nearest tree. "He's as agile, playful, and daring as me," says Sucha, discovering that her friend **is more like her than she thought.**

Yeah!

Who said that all princesses

must act and look the same? Sucha decides that when the time comes for her to be queen, she will rule in her own way, with her own style and personality.

Published in 2018 by **Windmill Books**, an Imprint of Rosen Publishing
29 East 21st Street, New York, NY 10010

Text: Aleix Cabrera | Illustration: Rocio Bonilla | Design and layout: Estudi Guasch, S.L.

CATALOGING-IN-PUBLICATION DATA

Names: Cabrera, Aleix.
Title: Princess Sucha's cat / Aleix Cabrera.
Description: New York : Windmill Books, 2018. | Series: Little princesses.
Identifiers: LCCN ISBN 9781508194606 (pbk.) | ISBN 9781508194002 (library bound) | ISBN 9781508194644 (6 pack) |
ISBN 9781508193951 (ebook)
Subjects: LCSH: Cats--Juvenile fiction. | Princesses--Juvenile fiction.
Classification: LCC PZ7.C334 Pri 2018 | DDC [E]--dc23

Manufactured in the United States of America
CPSIA Compliance Information: Batch BW18WM: For Further Information contact Rosen Publishing, New York, New York at 1-800-237-9932